PETS' PARTY

Books in the Animal Ark Pets Series

BEN M. BAGLIO

PETS' PARTY

Illustrations by
Paul Howard

Cover Illustration by
Chris Chapman

A
LITTLE APPLE
PAPERBACK

SCHOLASTIC INC.

New York Toronto London Auckland Sydney
Mexico City New Delhi Hong Kong Buenos Aires

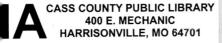

To Joseph Jack

Special thanks to Helen Magee

ISBN 0-439-23026-8

12 11 10   4 5 6/0

Printed in the U.S.A.   40
First Scholastic printing, November 2001

Contents

1

A New Boy at School

"Come on, James, the bell rang." Mandy Hope shivered as she called over her shoulder to her best friend. She could feel her cheeks glowing red. The wind was blowing cold off the moors that surrounded the village of Welford. Mandy was glad of the bright woolen scarf Grandma had knitted for her. It kept her cozy even in the chilliest of winds.

It's nearly Christmas, Mandy thought happily. Maybe there would be snow soon. James Hunter ran through the school gate behind her. As he went, he skidded on a patch of ice and bumped into a thin, elderly lady. She was muffled up in a long black coat and had a black felt hat pulled down over her ears.

"Sorry, Mrs. Trigg," James apologized.

Mrs. Trigg gave James a severe look. "Really, James, why weren't you looking where you were going?" she asked sternly.

"I slipped on some ice," James protested.

"You shouldn't have been running," Mrs. Trigg replied. "You children are always running everywhere. Max is just the same."

Max, Mandy thought. *Mrs. Trigg's grandson.* Mrs. Trigg lived in Holly Cottage, near Lilac Cottage where Mandy's grandma and grandpa lived. Mandy's grandma had told her that Max was coming to stay with his grandmother until after Christmas, because his dad was work-

ing overseas and his mom had gone into the hospital.

"Hello, Mrs. Trigg," Mandy said. "Has your grandson arrived yet?"

"I've just left him with his teacher," Mrs. Trigg replied. "He's going to be in Mrs. Todd's class."

Mandy nodded. "Mrs. Todd is my teacher, too," she said. "I'll look after Max if you like. James and I can introduce him to *everybody!*"

Mrs. Trigg smiled. "That would be very kind, Mandy," she said. "I thought it would do him good to spend the week before Christmas vacation at school with other children. *I* won't be much company for him."

Mandy smiled back, pleased. Mrs. Trigg hardly ever smiled; she usually looked worried. Mandy thought she seemed much nicer when she smiled.

"Isn't it great that Max is staying with you?" Mandy said. "I'm sure he'll enjoy it, too."

"I hope so," Mrs. Trigg replied. Then she sighed. "It's that dog of his that really worries me. It's going to be such trouble."

"Dog!" Mandy exclaimed. "He's brought a dog with him?" Mandy loved animals, which was just as well since her parents were vets in Welford. They lived in Animal Ark, a stone cottage with a clinic attached. Mandy loved meeting all her parents' animal patients.

"I've told Max the dog has to sleep in the garden shed," Mrs. Trigg went on. "I don't want all the mess and bother that pets make."

Mandy bit back her reply. Because Animal Ark was so busy with animal patients, Mandy wasn't allowed a pet for the time being, though she would have loved one. She couldn't imagine a pet ever being a bother.

"Come on, Mandy," James urged her. "The bell rang ages ago."

Mandy waved good-bye to Mrs. Trigg and raced into school. She couldn't wait to meet Max's dog. A cold gust of wind blew as she crossed the school yard. She shivered and pulled her soft, red scarf up to her chin. Imagine making a dog sleep in the garden shed in this weather. Poor thing!

"What's your dog's name?" Mandy asked Max at morning recess.

Everyone had crowded around Max, telling him all about Welford and trying to make him welcome.

"Sandy," Max replied. "He's a cairn terrier. My dad gave him to me before he went to work abroad. He's six months old now."

"So he's still a puppy!" Mandy exclaimed delightedly.

"Peter's got a cairn, too. He's called Timmy," James told Max.

"But Timmy's more of a *terror* than a *terrier*," Peter Foster added, grinning. "He's the naughtiest dog in Welford."

Max's big blue eyes lit up. "Cairns aren't really naughty," he said. "They've just got lots of energy. Maybe Sandy and Timmy could be friends."

"And James has a Labrador. His name is Blackie," Mandy told Max. "Blackie *loves* making friends with other dogs."

"I bet Blackie doesn't have to sleep in the garden shed," Max said.

"Of course he doesn't," James replied fiercely. Then he looked sympathetically at Max. "Your grandma told us that Sandy had to. Won't she let him into the house at all?"

Max shook his head. His eyes looked sad. "She thinks he would make too much of a mess."

Mandy felt very sorry for Max. "Why don't you bring Sandy around to Animal Ark?" she suggested. "And we can take him and Blackie out for walks. Blackie would love that, wouldn't he, James?"

James nodded. "And you can bring him carol singing the day before Christmas Eve," he added. "There will be loads of us going around the village, and everyone is going to bring their pets."

"I won't be able to bring Toto though," Jill Redfern said. "Toto is a tortoise and tortoises hibernate in winter."

"But I'm bringing Duchess, my Persian cat," said Richard Tanner.

"And I'm bringing Minnie, my mouse," Amy Fenton piped up. "Of course, I'll have to wrap her up warmly."

Mandy smiled and looked up at the sky. "Do you think there will be snow for Christmas?" she asked.

"I hope so," Max said. "At least then it will seem a bit more *like* Christmas." Then his face fell. "But then it might be too cold for Sandy in the garden shed."

Mandy looked at him in concern. "You

aren't unhappy at Holly Cottage, are you?" she asked.

Max looked at the floor, then back at Mandy. "Not really," he said. "I love my grandmother but it isn't like being home. Mom and Dad don't mind if Sandy jumps on the furniture or anything, but Grandma is so fussy about things like that. And she doesn't even have a Christmas tree. Mom and Dad and I decorate a Christmas tree every year and now I won't be with them for Christmas. Dad is working abroad, and he isn't sure if he'll be able to get

home for Christmas. And now Mom might not be home, either." Max looked even more sad.

"I'll tell you what," Mandy suggested. "James and I are going around to *my* grandma's after school. She lives at Lilac Cottage, close to your grandma's. Why don't we bring Blackie to meet Sandy afterward?"

"Would you?" asked Max. "I'd really like that — and so would Sandy."

"It's a date," said Mandy. "And, I promise you, Max, you're going to have a great Christmas in Welford. We'll make sure of it; won't we, everybody?" Mandy looked around at her friends. They all nodded in agreement.

"Of course we will," Gary Roberts said. "You can come and see Gertie, my garter snake, if you like."

"How would you like to have a ride on Paddy, my pony?" Paul Stevens asked.

Max laughed. "I'd love it," he replied. "Is Welford full of animals?"

"Just wait till you see Animal Ark," Mandy

told him. "At the moment we've got a parrot and a rabbit, two kittens and a gerbil, a hamster, a parakeet, and three guinea pigs."

"Wow!" said Max. "You're going to have a full house for Christmas."

Mandy shook her head. "Mom and Dad like to send as many animals as possible home at Christmas," she explained. "They're working really hard to get them all well enough to go back to their owners by Christmas Eve."

"I'll have to hurry if I want to see all the animals before they leave, then," said Max. "Can I really come to Animal Ark?"

"So long as you promise to bring Sandy," Mandy insisted.

"That's no problem," Max replied, smiling. "Sandy and I go everywhere together."

The bell rang for the end of recess and Mandy looked across at James. He gave her the thumbs-up sign. If it was up to Welford Village Elementary School, Max was going to have a very good Christmas indeed! But one thing still troubled Mandy. Sandy's Christmas would be no fun at all if Mrs. Trigg had anything to do with it. Mandy couldn't bear the thought of the poor puppy out in the cold garden shed on his own. She frowned. Somehow she had to change Mrs. Trigg's mind!

2

Meeting Sandy

"Just imagine it, Grandma!" Mandy wailed when she and James were at Lilac Cottage, having a snack. "Sandy has to sleep in the garden shed!"

"Now, now, Mandy," Grandpa put in. "I'm sure Maggie Trigg has a snug, warm bed for the little fellow. She's a kind woman. She would never be cruel to an animal."

"She's just very fussy," Grandma said, putting a plate of cheese sandwiches, and another one of homemade ginger cake, on the table.

James slipped a bit of cheese sandwich to Blackie. The Labrador pup gobbled it up and thumped his tail on the floor. At least *Blackie* was happy!

Mandy sighed. "Why doesn't Mrs. Trigg like animals, Grandma?"

Grandma shrugged. "I don't think Maggie dislikes animals," she replied. "I would imagine that she just thinks they make a lot of mess. You know, she used to be a rather jolly, happy-go-lucky sort of person. She used to enjoy coming to the Women's Club with me."

"And she used to be very involved in Welford's amateur dramatic society," Grandpa added.

"Mrs. Trigg?" exclaimed Mandy.

Grandpa nodded. "Maggie and her husband,

Bill, directed the Christmas play every year in the church hall," he went on. "But a few years ago Bill died, and since then Maggie seems to have lost interest in everything, poor woman."

"She doesn't get involved with anything anymore," Grandma agreed. "She spends all her time cleaning her house. It's as if she decided to put all her love and care into Holly Cottage."

"I think it will be good for Maggie to have Max staying with her," Grandpa said thoughtfully. "It'll give her someone else to care for."

"You could be right, Tom," Mandy's grandma replied. "I think she's lonely."

"So why doesn't she get a pet?" Mandy asked, helping herself to a large piece of ginger cake. "No, don't tell me — it would make too much of a mess." She sighed again. "Do you think Mrs. Trigg will ever change her mind about animals?"

Grandpa ruffled Mandy's short, fair hair. "Are you going to make a project out of Maggie Trigg?" he asked, his eyes twinkling.

Mandy stopped chewing for a moment.

"Maybe I will," she said. "Maybe that's *just* what I'll do."

James shoved his glasses up on his nose and rolled his eyes. "Uh-oh," he said. "Poor Mrs. Trigg."

"Poor Sandy!" Mandy retorted. Then she smiled. "Let's go! I can't wait to meet him!"

Mandy and James raced a few houses down the lane to Holly Cottage. Blackie bounded along beside them, enjoying the run.

"There's somebody in the garden shed," James said as they went through the gate.

Warm yellow light spilled out of the window of the garden shed onto the path. The winter afternoon was growing dark and the little shed looked cozy.

Max popped his head around the garden shed door as he heard their voices. "In here," he said. "Sandy is waiting for you."

Mandy ran toward the shed door and a furry bundle launched itself at her. "Oh, aren't you gorgeous!" she exclaimed as Sandy jumped up and put his two front paws on her legs. "I can see why you call him Sandy, Max."

The little terrier was a pale golden color. His shaggy coat looked thick and well groomed. Max obviously took very good care of his pet. Mandy bent down and fussed over Sandy, rubbing his ears. The puppy rolled over onto his back and she tickled his tummy.

Blackie scampered into the shed after James. The Labrador wagged his tail furiously when he saw Sandy.

"Hey, watch out!" Max said, grabbing a packet of seeds that Blackie's tail had knocked off a low shelf.

Blackie took no notice. He was already snuffling at Sandy's nose, butting the other pup playfully. Sandy sprang up and butted Blackie back. Soon the two dogs were rolling on the garden shed floor, playing and getting to know each other.

James laughed. "It looks like they're friends already," he remarked.

Max looked proudly at his pet. "Sandy just loves company," he said. "I hate leaving him in here on his own."

Mandy looked around the shed. There was a dog basket in one corner with a warm, woolen blanket inside. Beside it was a food bowl, a water bowl, and a hot-water bottle.

"I put the hot-water bottle there in case he gets cold during the night," Max told them.

Mandy looked at Max sympathetically. "You've made the shed really comfortable for him," she said. "I'm sure he'll be all right. Cairn terriers have lovely thick, warm coats."

Max's mouth drooped. "It's just that I'm so used to having him around," he explained. "What if he misses me during the night? He'll howl his head off. And what about during the day when I'm at school? Who's going to take him for a walk? He'll probably cry all day."

James frowned. "Your grandma won't like that," he said.

"Max!" called a voice from the back door of the cottage. "Max, where are you?"

"In the garden shed, Grandma," Max called back. "Mandy and James have come to visit Sandy."

Mrs. Trigg peered out from the kitchen door. "It's cold out there," she said. "Come inside." The old lady turned and went back into the house.

Blackie sat up, his ears pricked. Before James could stop him, the Labrador had galloped up the path and into the cottage.

"Uh-oh," said James. "Blackie, come back!"

Sandy gave a short bark and raced up the path after Blackie.

"Sandy!" Max shouted. But both dogs had disappeared.

Mandy, James, and Max all dived out through the door of the shed, hurtling up the path after the dogs. Mandy got to the kitchen door first, and winced as she heard a dreadful clatter.

Mrs. Trigg was standing in the middle of the kitchen, looking very annoyed. A pot rack had been overturned and the floor was littered with pots and pans. "*Now* do you see why I don't let dogs in the house, Max?" Mrs. Trigg said as he came into the kitchen with James. "Look what those dogs have done. I'm beginning to think it would be better to send Sandy to a kennel if he's going to behave like this."

Max gasped. "Oh, no, Grandma!" he pleaded as he bent to pick up the pots and pans. "Sandy didn't mean any harm. I'll clean this up. Please don't send him away."

Mrs. Trigg looked at Max's white, worried

face, and her own stern expression softened just a little. "Now, now," she said. "There's no need to get so upset over an animal, Max."

"But he isn't just an animal," Max protested. "He's *Sandy*. Dad gave him to me before he went to work abroad, and I promised Mom I would take good care of him while she was in the hospital. I'm all he's got just now!" Mandy could see that he was holding back his tears.

Mrs. Trigg looked shocked at Max's outburst. "Oh, dear," she sighed, ruffling her grandson's hair. "You're missing your mom and dad a lot, aren't you?" She didn't seem angry anymore.

Max nodded. "Do you think maybe Mom will be out of the hospital for Christmas?" he asked.

"I'm afraid not, Max," she said softly. "I called the hospital today, and they don't think that's very likely."

Max hung his head and Sandy reached up to him, licking his hand. "Oh, Sandy," Max said, burying his face in Sandy's neck.

Mrs. Trigg's expression softened as she looked

at Max and Sandy. "Don't worry about the kennel, Max," she said. "We'll manage somehow."

"You mean you won't send him away?" Max asked hopefully.

Mrs. Trigg sighed and set the pot rack upright. "Not if he behaves himself," she said at last, looking down at the puppy. Sandy put his head on one side and looked appealingly up at Mrs. Trigg. "Bad dog!" she said to him. But Mandy noticed the old lady couldn't help smiling a little as she helped Max replace the pots and pans.

Sandy scampered over to Mrs. Trigg and began trying to undo her shoelaces, wagging his stumpy tail. He put a paw on top of her left foot and rubbed his head against her ankle. Mandy was pleased to see that Mrs. Trigg didn't push the puppy away.

Max scooped him up. "I'll take him back to the garden shed," he said. "He'll be good, I promise, Grandma."

Mrs. Trigg shook her head. "Come near the fire and get warm first. You can take him out later. Leave him in here in the kitchen for now. Come on, all of you."

James looked at Mandy as Mrs. Trigg led the way out of the kitchen. "Where's Blackie?" he mouthed.

Mandy gasped. "I'd forgotten about Blackie," she confessed. "Where on earth has he gone to?"

3

Pets in Trouble!

Mrs. Trigg's voice floated back to them from the living room. "Well, of all the nerve!" she exclaimed.

Mandy and James hurried into the living room behind her. "Oh, no!" said James.

Blackie was stretched out on the sofa in front of the fire. His eyes were closed and he was snoozing peacefully. An embarrassed James collared Balckie and dragged him off.

"Just look at all the dog hairs over my sofa," Mrs. Trigg complained.

"Sorry, Mrs. Trigg," James apologized.

While Mrs. Trigg went to get a brush, Mandy cast a quick look around the living room. The fire burned brightly in the grate, but everything was too neat and tidy to be comfortable and welcoming. There wasn't a Christmas decoration in sight and, worst of all, no Christmas tree.

"I guess we'd better be going," Mandy said to Max.

Max nodded. "I'll see you tomorrow at school," he replied.

"Why don't you come to Animal Ark after school?" Mandy suggested as Mrs. Trigg came back into the room with a dustpan and brush. "Grandpa will walk over to Animal Ark with you; it's on the way. And bring Sandy. Then we can go to carol practice together afterward."

The carol singers had arranged a practice ses–

sion at the village hall. Mrs. Ponsonby had promised to supervise them, and coach them! Mrs. Ponsonby was chairwoman of the Welford Women's Club. She always liked to get involved in anything that was happening in the village. In fact, she usually reckoned she should be in charge.

"May I go with Sandy to Mandy's house after school tomorrow, Grandma?" Max asked. "Mandy's grandpa will walk me over there."

"Haven't your mom and dad got enough animals to look after, without Sandy getting under their feet?" Mrs. Trigg asked Mandy.

Mandy smiled. "Oh, no," she assured Mrs. Trigg. "They won't mind at all. They love animals — and they'll adore Sandy. He's so sweet."

Mrs. Trigg looked unsure. "I don't know about sweet," she said. "Animals just make a mess as far as I can see."

"But they're such good companions," Mandy went on. "Mrs. Ponsonby is always saying how lonely she would be without Pandora." Mrs. Ponsonby might be the bossiest woman in Welford, but she really loved Pandora, her Pekingese.

Mrs. Trigg looked thoughtful as she bent to brush the dog hairs off the sofa. James nudged Mandy and she followed his eyes. Sandy had crept into the room after Mrs. Trigg. He stretched a paw up to the low coffee table where Mrs. Trigg's knitting lay, neatly rolled up. Before Max could get to him he had loosened the ball of wool and it had dropped to the floor. Sandy scampered after it just as Mrs. Trigg turned around.

"No!" she said sternly to the little dog as he made to pounce on the ball of wool. "Sit!"

Sandy looked up at her, then sat down obediently, his head on one side. As Mrs. Trigg bent down to pick up her wool, the little dog lifted his right paw and held it out to her.

Mandy couldn't help smiling; he looked so adorable.

"That's a trick I taught him," Max said proudly. "He wants to shake hands Grandma."

"Hmmph," said Mrs. Trigg. Rather stiffly,

she quickly "shook hands" with Sandy, then wiped her hand on her apron. "You'd be better teaching him to do as he's told," she added.

"But he *did*, Mrs. Trigg," Mandy put in. "He sat down when you told him, and he hasn't even touched the ball of wool."

Mrs. Trigg stood with the dustpan and brush in her hand, looking at Sandy. "I suppose you're right, Mandy," she admitted. "He obviously recognizes a firm tone of voice."

James looked out of the window. "Oh, look!" he said. "It's started to snow. We can go sledding over the weekend if it sticks."

Mandy and Max rushed to the window. Big fat flakes of snow were falling, swirling in the light from the window.

"Isn't it lovely?" Mandy breathed. "It's so *Christmassy!*"

"But it makes a terrible mess when it melts," Mrs. Trigg said.

Mandy looked at the old woman. Her dark navy cardigan was buttoned right up to the neck and the white collar of her blouse was crisp and neat. Her skirt was dark and neat, too. Even her apron looked as if it had been starched and pressed. Everything about her was neat and buttoned-up. Her short gray hair was tucked behind her ears — neatly!

"But the snow is beautiful while it lasts, Mrs. Trigg," Mandy said. "Don't you think so?"

Mrs. Trigg came to stand beside them. She turned her face up to watch the snowflakes falling. "Your grandpa used to love snow, Max," she said softly. "You probably don't remember, but when you were a very little boy he made a snowman with you out in the garden, there."

Mandy looked at Mrs. Trigg. Her face was softer somehow — as if she was remembering a lot of happy things.

Sandy had scampered up to join them. Max picked him up and looked up at his grandma. "I remember," he said. "Grandpa made me the best snowman in the world." Mrs. Trigg put her arm around her grandson's shoulder and hugged him.

"We'd better go," Mandy said quietly.

"Should I take Sandy out to the garden shed now?" Max asked his grandma reluctantly.

Sandy lifted his head and licked Mrs. Trigg's hand. The old woman drew her hand away, wiping it on her apron again. But then she said briskly, "Maybe we'd better let him sleep in the warm kitchen tonight."

"Oh, thanks, Grandma!" Max said, his face lighting up.

Mrs. Trigg smiled at her grandson. "But I won't have him in the rest of the house," she warned. "I can't stand all these dog hairs around," she said, giving Blackie a stern look.

Mandy and James grinned at each other. Max was cuddling Sandy as if he would never let him go, and Mrs. Trigg was bustling about, sweeping up more invisible dog hairs.

"Come on, Blackie," James said. "Let's go home. See you tomorrow, Max."

*　　*　　*

The carol singers gathered in the village hall the following afternoon. James and Max had brought Blackie and Sandy, and Peter Foster had turned up with Timmy, his cairn terrier. The others had left their pets at home until the big day. Mrs. Ponsonby couldn't complain about the dogs being there: She had brought Pandora.

"*Hark! The herald angels sing . . .*" sang the carol singers.

Mrs. Ponsonby stood in front of them, waving her arms around. "Louder!" she boomed. "*Glory to the newborn King!*" Her voice wavered on the high notes and Mandy suppressed a giggle. Blackie began to howl as Mrs. Ponsonby's voice wobbled through the carol.

"At least Mrs. Ponsonby isn't coming out carol singing with us," Gary Roberts said, grinning.

"Don't count on it," Jill Redfern replied.

"*Peace on earth, and mercy mild,*" Mandy sang. She gave Jill a dig in the ribs and Jill joined in.

"*God and sinners reconciled,*" the carolers roared.

Blackie scampered over to where Pandora was sitting behind her owner. The Pekingese was watching the carol singers and joining in now and again with short, sharp yelps. Blackie gave Pandora a nudge with his nose and Pandora yelped even more.

Mrs. Ponsonby turned. "Blackie!" she thundered. The Labrador took off and streaked under a chair.

James made a dive for Blackie as Mrs. Ponsonby scooped Pandora up and clasped her pet to her chest.

"Sorry, Mrs. Ponsonby," James apologized as the carol singing drifted to a stop.

"Really, James," Mrs. Ponsonby scolded. "If you can't keep that dog of yours under control, you shouldn't bring him to rehearsals. Oh, my poor darling," Mrs. Ponsonby murmured to Pandora. "Did that wicked Blackie upset you?"

Pandora sneezed, jumped out of Mrs. Ponsonby's arms, and raced off behind the piano. Sandy scampered after her and Mrs. Ponsonby let out a screech.

"Pandora must *not* be overexcited," she declared. "My little angel is so highly strung."

"Whoops!" said Peter Foster as Timmy shot off after the other dogs. Peter made a lunge for his pet, but Timmy managed to slip out of his grasp. The dogs had clearly had enough carol singing for the day; they wanted to play. In no time at all, they were rolling around and chasing one another.

"Look at them!" said Max delightedly. "They're having a great time."

"They're leading my precious Pandora astray," Mrs. Ponsonby wailed as she waded into the midst of the dogs, scattering them in all directions. Blackie bumped into a chair and it fell over, spilling song sheets on the floor.

"What a noise!" a voice said from the door. "I thought Mrs. Ponsonby was in charge."

Mandy swung around. Mrs. Trigg stood there, looking very disapproving. Mandy looked at her watch; it must be time to go. Mrs. Trigg had insisted on coming to get Max. She took the responsibility of looking after him very seriously and always seemed worried in case anything should happen to him while he was in her care.

"I *am* in charge, Maggie," Mrs. Ponsonby declared, coming out from behind the piano. Her face was as red as the pompom on her hat. She had been chasing after Pandora. At that moment, Pandora scampered up to her and Mrs.

Ponsonby bent down and picked up her pet. Carol sheets were scattered on the floor and several more chairs had been overturned.

Max wrestled a rather chewed sheet of music from Sandy and handed it back to Mrs. Ponsonby. "Sorry, Mrs. Ponsonby," he said.

Mrs. Ponsonby took the soggy piece of paper. "Don't worry about it, my dear! We've got plenty." The carolers cheerfully continued cleaning up.

Mrs. Trigg looked around and sniffed. "Animals!" she said. "What a mess they cause!"

Sandy gave a short bark and shot across the room to Mrs. Trigg, wagging his tail furiously. No matter what Mrs. Trigg thought of Sandy, the little dog loved *her*.

"Hmmph!" said Mrs. Trigg when Sandy sat down almost on top of her boots and thumped his stumpy tail. "I see *you've* been naughty, too," she said sternly, looking down at the little dog. But Mandy noticed that she bent to give him a quick pat.

Mrs. Trigg shook her head at Mrs. Ponsonby. "It seems to me that pets are nothing but trouble," she announced.

Mrs. Ponsonby drew herself up. "I can't agree with you, Maggie," she declared. "Pandora is very well behaved — usually. And she is such a good companion to me. I wouldn't be without her for the world. I'm never lonely with my Pandora around."

Pandora settled down in Mrs. Ponsonby's arms, rubbing her head against her owner's hand.

Mrs. Trigg looked at the little dog. "Well, there *is* that," she agreed. "Sometimes I do get lonely," she added softly.

"Then you really should think about having a pet, Maggie," Mrs. Ponsonby said briskly. "You'd never feel alone if you had a little dog like my Pandora to keep you company. Didn't I see you walking Sandy this morning?"

Mrs. Trigg flushed. "Max was at school," she explained. "Sandy needed a walk."

"That's another thing about dogs," Mrs. Pon-

sonby continued. "They get you out of the house — you would meet people. You spend far too much time cleaning that cottage of yours, my dear. Why don't you come back to the Women's Club? You used to enjoy it so much and you need to get out more!"

With that, Mrs. Ponsonby turned away and began to shepherd the children into their coats and hats.

Mrs. Trigg looked after her. "Well, really!" she said, her face rather red.

Mandy came to stand beside Mrs. Trigg. "Mrs. Ponsonby bosses *everybody* around," she said sympathetically. "But she's right about one thing, Mrs. Trigg. Pets can be wonderful company."

"Hmmph!" said Mrs. Trigg. "They can also be a lot of hard work. Come along, Max."

Mandy watched as Mrs. Trigg bustled Max and Sandy out of the door. Mrs. Trigg might have taken Sandy for a walk, but that didn't mean she like dogs. It wasn't going to be easy changing Mrs. Trigg's mind about pets!

4

An Abandoned Puppy

"I think it's going to snow again," Dr. Adam said on Saturday morning as he came into the residential unit at Animal Ark. It had snowed a lot in the last few days. The snow lay deep and thick on the moors around Welford and there were drifts piled high against the hedges in some of the streets. Even the village square was totally white, and the branches of the surrounding trees were covered in snow.

It was so cold, Mandy had found icicles hanging outside her bedroom window that morning. She had hurried downstairs to put out fresh nuts and bacon rind for the birds; it wasn't easy for them to find food with this much snow around. There would certainly be enough snow for sledding, as long as there wasn't a sudden thaw.

"I hope it snows all day and all night," she said happily. "We're planning to go sledding tomorrow." She had a tiny kitten in her arms. It had swallowed a plastic bottle top, which had lodged in the young animal's throat. Dr. Adam had needed to sedate the kitten before he could remove it.

"I love sledding," said James, who had arrived after breakfast. "When is Max coming over, Mandy?"

Mandy put the kitten back in its cage. "Any time now," she replied, tickling the little animal under its chin. "He's coming to help choose

the Christmas tree. Since he can't have one at Holly Cottage, I thought he could help decorate ours." It was now Christmas vacation — time to put up the Animal Ark Christmas tree!

"I saw Max's grandma out walking Sandy again yesterday," Dr. Adam said. "She seemed to be getting on really well with him — much better than she was earlier in the week."

Mandy smiled. "She's been taking him for walks while Max has been at school," she told her father. "She won't have to do that over the Christmas holidays, of course."

Dr. Adam put his head on one side, looking thoughtful. "Mmm," he said. "Pity. She looked as if she was really enjoying it."

"Mrs. Ponsonby told her she should get a dog," Mandy said.

Dr. Adam laughed. "It isn't often you and Mrs. Ponsonby agree on anything!"

"Oh, but I think *everybody* should have animals in their life," Mandy declared. "Just look at Max and Sandy."

Max and Sandy had been regular visitors to Animal Ark over the last few days. Max loved seeing the animals, and Sandy had made good friends with Blackie.

"We should get this little fellow home in time for Christmas," Dr. Adam remarked, looking at the kitten.

Mandy bent down and smiled at the kitten. "No more bottle tops," she warned. She glanced around the other cages. Only the gerbil and the hamster remained now; the other animals had all gone back to their owners. Mandy was always glad to see animals get well enough to go home, but she missed them when they left.

"I've called George Fenton," Dr. Adam went on. "He says you can go and choose a tree any time, and I'll pay for it next time I'm passing by."

Mr. Fenton was Amy's dad. He owned a sawmill just on the edge of the village, and at Christmas he turned his workshop into a Christmas tree shop.

"Can I choose a really big one, Dad?" Mandy asked.

Dr. Emily, Mandy's mom, came through the door just as Mandy was speaking. "Just make sure it'll fit in the living room," she said, her green eyes twinkling. "We don't want to have to chop the top off."

"I've measured it," Mandy replied. "We can get a six-foot tree and still have room to put the star on top!"

"Wow!" said Dr. Emily. "It's just as well you've got Paddy to help bring that home."

Mandy grinned. "We're going to take my

sled," she told her mother. "Paul has been practicing with Paddy. He says his pony just loves pulling a sled — and he's very strong."

"There's Max!" James called, looking out of the window. "Let's go, Mandy."

Mandy glanced outside. The garden was already carpeted in fresh snow. The snowman that she, James, and Max had made yesterday stood in the middle of the lawn. There was a covering of snow on the carrot they had used for a nose.

"Wrap up warmly," Dr. Emily called after them as they raced out of the residential unit.

Mandy and James shrugged themselves into heavy jackets, crammed woolen hats on their heads, and thrust their hands into gloves. Blackie rushed out from behind the reception desk to meet them.

"Thanks for looking after him," James said to Jean Knox, the receptionist. Blackie wasn't allowed into the residential unit with the sick animals.

Jean looked over her glasses at James. "Any

time, James," she replied. "He's good company."

Mandy put her head on one side. "I wish Mrs. Trigg thought dogs were good company," she said.

"Oh, knowing you, Mandy, you'll persuade her." Jean laughed, nodding her head. Her glasses slid off her nose and bounced on the end of their chain.

"Maybe I will," Mandy said thoughtfully. "You know, she's still letting Sandy sleep in the kitchen because it's been snowing so much. She says she can mop the floor every day."

"That's a lot better than the garden shed for Sandy," Jean agreed.

Mandy opened the door and Sandy threw himself at her. She bent down to let him lick her face in welcome. Blackie bounded out of the door, and the two dogs rolled on the ground, chasing each other and kicking up great flurries of soft, powdery snow.

"Christmas tree time!" Max said happily.

Mandy smiled. She was *really* glad she had

suggested that Max help choose the tree. He seemed so excited about decorating it.

"Here, Blackie," she called, clipping on Blackie's leash as the Labrador bounded up to her.

"I've got the sled," James called, dragging a red sled off the porch. "Let's go!"

First they had to go and get Paul and Paddy from Paul's house. They roped the sled to the harness they had rigged up for Paddy. Blackie gave a short bark and leaped onto the sled.

Sandy followed, jumping on behind the Labrador.

Paul grinned as James tried to shoo the dogs off. "Leave them," he said. "It's good practice for Paddy."

As they walked down the main street, they made quite a picture. Mr. and Mrs. McFarlane came out of the post office to watch.

"Are you playing Santa Claus?" Mr. McFarlane called to them.

"Paddy makes a good Rudolph, but where's his red nose?" Mrs. McFarlane joked.

They laughed and waved. As they passed the Fox and Goose, Mr. Hardy, the landlord, came out to watch. "You need some jingle bells," he remarked, smiling.

Mandy looked at Paddy. The sturdy little Exmoor pony really was enjoying pulling the sled.

Paul had got Paddy from a rescue sanctuary. The little pony had been very badly treated. The first time Mandy saw him, he had been in such poor condition that he wouldn't even have been able to pull a sled. Now his coat was a glossy grayish brown and his eyes were clear and bright — not sad, the way they had been when Mandy first saw him at the sanctuary.

As Mandy watched, Paddy's head went up and he shook his dark-brown mane, his breath cloudy on the frosty air. Paul had done a wonderful job with Paddy — and Paddy had loved Paul right from the start.

Mandy laid a hand on Paddy's warm winter coat. "Good boy, Paddy!" she said softly. "Good boy!"

Soon they were out of the village and heading toward the sawmill.

Mandy saw Amy perched on the gate as they turned into the driveway. She stood up, clutching the gate with one mittened hand and waving to them with the other. The bright yellow pompoms on her woolen hat danced merrily as she called out to them. "I've told Dad to show you all the best trees," she told them, swinging the gate open.

Paddy plodded through the gate into the yard, and Mr. Fenton came out of the shed.

"Come in," he called. "Let's go and choose your tree. Then you can have some apple pie while I rope it onto the sled for you."

Mandy and the others followed him excitedly into the shed. The smell of resin and pine needles filled the space. Mandy gazed at the forest of trees propped up against the walls. There were so many to choose from, and each one they looked at seemed better than the last.

Finally, the perfect tree was chosen. "That one!" Max said, pointing to a large, glossy fir tree. The branches of the tree he had selected were feathery and full. Best of all, it had a long, straight top branch.

"Perfect for the Christmas star," Mandy said, smiling happily.

James and Paul nodded in agreement.

"Good choice, Max," James said as he waved to Mr. Fenton.

Mandy looked at Max's shining face. He might not have a tree at Holly Cottage, but choosing the one for Animal Ark was surely the next best thing!

"Amy's mom's apple pie was great," James said as they slowly made their way back down the road toward Animal Ark.

Mandy laughed. "She promised to have some more ready for us when we go carol singing," she said.

Paul was leading Paddy, guiding the pony carefully over the rough trail. Mandy looked up as a large snowflake settled on her nose. "Dad was right!" she exclaimed. "He said it would snow again."

"I wonder if the pond at the bottom of Beacon Hill will be frozen," James said.

"Where's that?" asked Max.

Mandy pointed across the fields to a snow-topped hill. "Over there," she said. "It's a great hill for sledding, and sometimes, if it's really cold, the pond at the bottom freezes over and we can skate on it.

"You have to be careful, though," Paul warned. "The pond is part of the river and the ice has to be really, *really* solid before you try skating."

"Sledding will be enough for me," Max said happily. "You know, Welford is a really great place. We've got a park near where I live, but nothing like this. It must be great living in the country all the time."

Mandy smiled and lifted her face to the snowflakes. "It is," she agreed. "I can't imagine living anywhere else but Welford."

Paddy's hooves were beginning to make marks in the newly fallen snow, and the sled ran smoothly over the snowy ground. The tree, securely roped on, brushed its branches against Mandy's legs as she walked and the two dogs started chasing snowflakes. If the snow kept up, it was going to be a perfect Christmas.

They turned out of the trail onto the back road that ran between the Fentons' sawmill and Welford. Suddenly Sandy stopped at the edge of the ditch that bordered the road. Hanging over the ditch was a thorny bush, heavy with snow.

"Watch the thorns don't prick you, Sandy," Max warned.

Sandy turned his head toward his young master but wouldn't come away from the ditch. He stood there, legs stiff, tail erect, sniffing and growling softly.

"Come on, Sandy," Max said.

But the little dog stayed where he was and began to bark urgently.

Max frowned. "What is it, boy?" he asked.

Sandy looked up at him, still barking.

Max gazed down into the ditch. Then he reached out a gloved hand and moved a branch aside. "Oh, no!" he cried out. "Come and look at this."

Mandy hurried over, alerted by the note of shock in Max's voice. "What is it?" she asked. Then she saw for herself, and her heart began to beat faster.

There, lying huddled in the ditch beneath the thorn bush, was a little puppy. Its coat was

dark, but it was fast being covered with snow. And it wasn't moving.

Mandy felt her breath come back in a rush. Then she scrambled down into the ditch and lifted the puppy carefully. She breathed a sigh of relief as, through her gloves, she felt some warmth coming from the puppy's small body. It was alive.

But then Mandy caught sight of the snow where the puppy had lain. She gasped. It was red with blood. There was more blood on her gloves.

She called to the others. "It's a puppy. It's alive — but it's hurt. Bleeding. We've got to get it to Animal Ark as quickly as possible!"

James reached down and took the puppy gently from her. Mandy scrambled out of the ditch, unwrapping her scarf from her neck. "Here," she said. "Wrap this around it. We've got to keep it warm. The poor little thing looks as if it's been there a long time. It's unconscious."

When Mandy muffled the puppy up in her scarf, the little animal opened its eyes and let out a weak cry.

"Oh, the poor little thing," Max said. "It must be in real pain."

Mandy nodded. "The sooner we get back to Animal Ark, the better."

5

Safe at Animal Ark

Mandy gazed anxiously at the little puppy as it lay on the examination table at Animal Ark. "How is it?" she asked her mother.

Dr. Emily smiled as she finished cleaning the wound on the puppy's leg. "It's a *she*," she said. "I think she's going to be all right. She looks worse than she is, with the fur shaved off around her wound, but it will soon grow back. She is in shock and badly bruised, too, but you got to her just in time, Mandy. Another fifteen minutes in that ditch and she would have died from the cold.

"Sandy found her," Mandy told her mother.

Dr. Emily looked at Max's worried face as he stood on the other side of the examination table. "Then Sandy is a very clever puppy," she said. "Let's go and congratulate him."

Dr. Emily settled the injured puppy comfortably in one of the cages in the residential unit, with a warm blanket tucked around her. "There," Dr. Emily said. "A good sleep and she'll be as right as rain — except for her leg. We'll have to keep an eye on that."

"She won't be lame, will she?" James asked.

Dr. Emily shook her head. "It isn't as bad as that," she assured him. "The puppy should be ready to leave us in a few days."

"But she hasn't got a home," Mandy said.

"She doesn't even have a collar. And she's so tiny. How old is she, Mom?"

"About five months," Dr. Emily replied. "I'll be able to examine her better tomorrow, but I'd say she's probably had all her vaccinations."

"How do you think she got into the ditch, Dr. Emily?" James asked.

Mandy's mom looked serious. "I think she was abandoned," she said. "It happens sometimes. People get a puppy and forget that they are a lot of work. Then they take them out into the country and just let them go."

"But she was *hurt*," Mandy protested.

Dr. Emily looked sympathetically at Mandy. "Sometimes people just throw the pup out of a moving car," she explained. "It's a terrible thing to do, but at least this little puppy has been saved — thanks to you all."

Mandy shook her head. *How could anyone be so cruel?* "Oh, I promised I'd phone Paul," she said. "He had to take Paddy home and he's really worried about the puppy."

"You do that," Dr. Emily said. "Then we can cheer ourselves up by decorating the Christmas tree."

Max's face lit up. "May I stay and help?" he asked.

Mandy turned to him as they went out of the door. "Of course you may," she declared. "You're the chief tree decorator this year!"

Blackie and Sandy bounded over to them as they went into the reception area. Max grinned and bent down to give Sandy a cuddle. "And you're a hero, Sandy," he said.

Blackie gave a short bark. "See," said James. "Blackie thinks so as well."

"I wonder if Holly will like the tree," Max said.

"Holly?" asked Dr. Emily.

Max blushed. "Oh, that's what I was calling the puppy we rescued — just to myself. It's sort of Christmassy, don't you think?"

"I think Holly's a great name," Mandy agreed when she came back from making her phone call to Paul. She turned to her mother. "What will happen to her?" she asked.

"She'll have to go to the ASPCA once she's better," Dr. Emily replied. "It should only be a few days — Christmas Eve at the latest."

Mandy frowned. "But then nobody would be able to adopt her until after Christmas, Mom," she said. "You know how many puppies are abandoned then. It will be really hard for them to find her a home."

Dr. Emily sighed. "I know," she said. "But what else can we do? I can't send her to the

60

ASPCA until her leg is better. They have a lot of work already and, besides, they wouldn't allow anyone to adopt her until her leg had healed."

Mandy raised her head. "*We* could find her a home," she said. "We could find somebody here in Welford to take her."

Dr. Emily laughed. "I wouldn't put it past you, Mandy," she said. "Now, how about putting up that Christmas tree before Holly wakes up?"

Mandy, James, and Max quickly set to work covering the stand for the tree with some bright Christmas paper.

Dr. Adam arrived just as they finished. He had been out visiting one of the local farms, and his beard was dusted with snow. "It's snowing again," he said, moving toward the fire. "It's freezing out there."

"Do you think it's cold enough for the pond at the bottom of Beacon Hill to ice over?" James asked.

"I would imagine so," Dr. Adam replied.

But Mandy wasn't thinking of ice skating. She plunged straight into their story about Holly, dragging her father into the residential unit to see the puppy. Dr. Adam bent down to look at the sleeping pup. Holly was curled up, cozy and warm in her blanket. She was fast asleep, her nose twitching. Now and again she made soft snuffling noises.

"What breed is she, Dad?" Mandy whispered.

"She looks like some sort of terrier-cross to me," Dr. Adam replied. "A pretty little thing," he added, smiling. "Terriers — especially cross-breeds — are tough little things. No wonder Holly survived her ordeal."

"Well, she's safe now," Mandy breathed. "With people who will be kind to her," she added.

Dr. Adam ruffled his daughter's hair. "Come on," he said. "Let's leave her to sleep. We can bring her out later to see the Christmas tree."

*   *   *

"Oh, isn't it beautiful!" Mandy exclaimed, gazing at the Christmas tree. The dark-green branches shimmered in the firelight, giving out a wonderful scent in the heat of the room.

"It'll look even more beautiful when it's decorated," Dr. Emily said, coming into the room with a huge cardboard box in her hands. Blackie and Sandy followed at her heels. The dogs had been banned from the living room while Dr. Adam was putting up the tree. Now they stopped, side by side, and looked at the tree, sniffing the pinecones. Sandy launched himself at the tree and Max made a leap for him.

"Leave him," said Dr. Adam.

Max drew back, puzzled. Sandy rushed at the tree. As the prickly branches caught his nose, he jumped back, his head low. Cautiously he moved forward again, testing the needles on the branches. Then he sneezed.

"I think he'll keep his distance now." Dr. Emily laughed.

Max laughed, too. "This is Sandy's first Christmas," he said.

"So let's make it a really good one," Mandy announced, rummaging in the decorations box. "Look! I've found the star for the top of the tree!"

Half an hour later, Dr. Adam moved the stepladder away from the tree. Outside, the afternoon had grown dark. The light from the fire lit up the glittering ornaments, the sparkly tinsel, and the candy canes hanging from the tree's branches. Dr. Adam plugged in the tree lights. "Who's going to switch them on, then?" he asked.

Mandy spun around, a wide smile on her lips. "Max," she said.

Max walked slowly over to the switch and pressed it down. The tiny white bulbs sprang into life, dancing on the shiny decorations and glowing against the darkness outside.

"Wow!" said James. "That is just the *best* tree ever!"

Sandy and Blackie crept closer to the tree, ly-

ing down under it and gazing up at the twinkling lights.

"Now it *really* feels like Christmas," Mandy
said, smiling happily.

"And I smell apple pie," James added.

Everybody laughed. "Trust James!" said Dr.
Emily. "Come on, you all; you deserve a treat after all your hard work. Apple pie for everyone."

6

Sandy in Danger

"Holly is looking much better today," Dr. Emily told Mandy the next day as she examined the little pup.

"Isn't she beautiful?" Mandy said as Holly looked up at Dr. Emily and gave her hand a trusting lick. The puppy's little face looked adorable. "Why on earth would anyone abandon her? She's perfect."

"Who knows?" said her mother. "The important thing is that she's a fine, healthy pup and her leg will soon be better."

"When do you think her bandage can come off, Mom?" Mandy asked.

"Tomorrow," Dr. Emily told her. "The wound wasn't very deep, and it's healing nicely."

"But we don't have to send her away yet, do we?" Mandy asked.

Dr. Emily shook her head. "I'd like to keep her for a few more days, just to make sure she isn't suffering from delayed shock. She's still very young and she must have had quite a fright."

Mandy frowned. "But it'll be Christmas in three days," she said.

"Don't worry," Dr. Emily said. "We won't put her out in the snow."

Mandy smiled. "Oh, I know *that*, Mom," she

said. She looked out of the window. "James and Max and I are sledding on Beacon Hill this morning.

Dr. Emily rose from the table. "I wish I could come with you. It's been years since I've gone sledding."

"Why don't you?" Mandy asked.

Dr. Emily smiled. "Because I've got patients to see," she said. "Now, remember: get dressed —"

"Warmly," Mandy finished, grinning. "We will."

"Shh!" said Max to Mandy and James when they arrived at Holly Cottage. He was smiling.

"What is it?" whispered James.

Max put a finger to his lips and led them toward the living room door. It was open slightly and Mandy and James peered into the room. Mrs. Trigg was sitting on the sofa in front of the fire, dozing — and beside her, curled up at her side, was Sandy.

"What is she going to say when she wakes up?" Mandy whispered, grinning.

Max shook his head. "Grandma said Sandy could come into the living room because the weather was so cold," he explained.

"So she's getting to like him?" James asked.

"She won't admit it," Max said. "But I think she is. Only I don't know what she's going to say if she wakes and finds that Sandy has crept up to sit beside her — on the sofa!"

Just at that moment, a log shifted in the fire

and Mrs. Trigg stirred. Her hand went out and touched Sandy's neck. Sandy lifted his head and licked her hand.

Mrs. Trigg's eyes flew open and she looked down at the little dog. "Well, really, Sandy!" she said sternly. "Get down at once."

Sandy looked up at her and snuggled closer, clearly delighted at having sneaked up beside Mrs. Trigg. Mandy watched in amazement as the old lady's mouth curved in a reluctant smile.

"Bad dog," Mrs. Trigg said. But this time she didn't say it as if she meant it. She stood up and brushed her hands down her apron. "Look what you've done, Sandy," she scolded. "Now I've got dog hairs on my apron."

Sandy jumped down off the sofa and wagged his tail, then he rubbed his head against Mrs. Trigg's ankles and nibbled at her shoelaces.

"Silly little dog," Mrs. Trigg said, bending down and giving him a pat. "Shoo! I've got work to do."

Mandy, James, and Max looked at one another. Maybe Sandy was winning Mrs. Trigg over after all!

The sun was shining on the crisp, white snow as Mandy, James, and Max made their way to Beacon Hill. Mandy looked at the pond at the foot of the hill. "We could try skating another day," she said. "The ice looks firm enough."

Blackie gave a short bark and raced on ahead toward the pond.

Sandy followed, overtaking Blackie and rolling in the snow in front of him. The two dogs leaped and rolled together. They were having a great time.

"They love playing together, don't they?" Max said.

James smiled. "The best of friends," he agreed as Blackie dived into a snowdrift and started kicking up enormous clouds of snow.

Sandy scampered out of range, waiting for his pal to reappear out of the snowdrift. As Mandy watched, she saw Sandy go very still and turn toward the pond, as if he had just heard something.

Mandy looked across the shining sheet of ice but couldn't see anything. "What's Sandy doing?" she asked Max.

Max shrugged. "Maybe he heard a bird or a rabbit," he said.

Mandy nodded. "Oh, look at Blackie!" She giggled.

Blackie burst out of the snowdrift, shaking snow in great dollops from his coat.

"It's a snowstorm!" James yelled.

Blackie barked and began to race past Sandy, towards the frozen pond beyond.

As Blackie ran toward the pond, Sandy turned and gave chase, running at Blackie and growling. The Labrador steered clear of him, keeping away from the pond.

Max frowned. "What on earth is Sandy doing?" he asked. "He's never done that before!"

Blackie ran toward the terrier again, trying to get around him, but Sandy stood his ground, his teeth bared.

"Sandy!" Max called. "Stop that!"

James ran ahead and grasped Blackie's collar. At once Sandy relaxed, coming to Max and wagging his tail.

"What was all that about?" Max asked, puzzled. "They usually get along so well together."

James shrugged. "Sandy seems all right now," he said. "Come on, let's go sledding."

They trudged up to the top of the hill.

"Race you to the bottom!" James yelled, pushing his sled off from the top of Beacon Hill.

"That's not fair — you've got a head start." Mandy called after him as she pushed her own sled off.

The snow was deep and soft. Mandy's sled skimmed over it, sending up flurries of powdery snow as she went. The sky was a clear blue and, below, the frozen pond was silver in the winter sun.

"Wait for me," called Max, behind her.

Mandy turned to watch as Max launched himself down the slope. When she turned back, she shouted, "James! Get out of the way!"

James, in front of her, turned around briefly as Mandy's sled shot down the hill. But he was too late; Mandy was going to crash into him. James turned his sled wildly, trying to get out of her path. Blackie bounded past downhill with Sandy at his heels. The dogs were having a wonderful time.

"Uh-oh!" Mandy said, dragging on the ropes of her sled as she hurtled toward James.

Max took a wide sweep to avoid them both. "See you at the bottom," he called as Mandy's sled crashed into James's. The two sleds overturned, tipping Mandy and James out into the snow. Mandy sat up, laughing, as James dived headfirst into a snowdrift.

"Are you all right?" she spluttered.

James's head appeared, covered in snow. He clambered back on to his sled. "I'll *still* race you!" he said.

But Mandy wasn't listening. Down near the pond at the bottom of the hill, Sandy was barking furiously. "Look!" Mandy exclaimed. "Sandy is acting oddly again."

As Max's sled made its way downhill, the little dog ran up to meet it, running right in its path. Max turned his sled desperately trying to avoid Sandy. For a few moments, his sled ran along the side of the hill and Sandy slowed down. Max steered his sled downward again. But again Sandy ran in front of him, barking furiously.

The ice on the pond gleamed in the sunshine. As they watched, Max once more turned his sled sharply to avoid Sandy. This time the sled overturned and he fell out onto the snow. But Sandy was going too fast to stop. The little dog skidded on the edge of the ice and shot out on to the surface of the pond, scrabbling wildly to keep his balance.

"Oh, no!" Mandy cried. "Look, James!" The ice beneath Sandy was beginning to crack.

Sandy scrabbled desperately for a footing on the slippery surface. Max got up and began to race toward his pet.

"No, Max! Wait!" James yelled. "The ice is cracking!"

Mandy and James pushed off their sled, racing downhill. Mandy got there first and grabbed Max. "You can't go out there," she gasped. "The ice won't support your weight. We could see cracks all over the pond from farther up the hill."

Max's face was white. "But what about Sandy?" he asked. "If the ice gives way, he'll drown!"

7

Rescue!

"What are we going to do?" James asked. Blackie strained forward; he wanted to help Sandy. James kept a tight hold on his collar.

Mandy frowned, thinking hard. Then an idea came to her. "We've got the sleds," she said. "We can lay one of them down at the edge of the ice where it's thickest. It would be like a platform. And the sleds are plastic; they aren't heavy."

"I think mine is even lighter than yours, Mandy," James said.

"That's it then," said Max. "If you two hold on to the sled, I can crawl out and try to reach Sandy."

"You?" Mandy sounded surprised.

Max looked at her seriously. "Sandy *is* my dog," he said.

Mandy glanced quickly at the puppy out on the ice. He was about two yards from the bank; cracks were spreading out around him. There was no time to lose and no time to argue.

"Right," she said. "You go on, Max. We'll pull the sled in if the ice cracks under you."

"Stay, Blackie!" James ordered.

The Labrador looked up at him worriedly, but didn't move even when James let go of his collar.

Quickly, Mandy and James laid James's sled down on the ice at the edge of the pond and Max began to crawl along the makeshift platform. The ice groaned under him and Mandy held her breath, watching the boy edge out toward his pet. She and James hung on tightly to the end of the sled. There was a sudden snap as a large piece of ice farther out broke loose and turned on its side. It floated for a moment before breaking up.

"That water will be really cold," James said worriedly.

Mandy nodded and bent down, ready to pull in the sled if necessary.

Max looked back. "I don't know if I can reach him," he said.

Mandy watched while Max inched his way along the sled as far as he could go. He was as close to Sandy as he could get now.

Sandy was gazing at Max, but Max couldn't reach him. Even with his arms outstretched, Sandy was still about eight inches away from Max. Max stretched out a hand. "Come on, Sandy," he coaxed. "Jump for it. Jump onto the sled."

There was another groan and then a loud crack. Mandy saw the ice under Sandy crack right across. Sandy's paws scrabbled at the ice under him as it split from side to side, leaving a great, gaping hole. Then he lost his balance, tumbling into the water. Max made a lunge and the breath stopped in Mandy's throat as the sled wobbled on the very edge of the ice hole.

"Max!" she yelled.

But Max wasn't listening; Sandy had disap- peared beneath the water. There was a flurry and the little dog appeared, struggling to stay afloat.

Blackie wanted to rush forward onto the ice, but James caught his collar. "No, boy," he said. "I know you want to help, but we can't have two of you out there."

"Don't let him sink under the ice," Mandy muttered, her eyes on Sandy. "He'd be trapped. Swim, Sandy, swim!"

As if he heard her, Sandy started to doggy paddle toward Max. Another raft of ice floated toward him, grazing his side, pushing him farther away from Max and forcing him underwater.

Max made a final grab, plunging his hand into the water as Sandy disappeared again. Then, with a heave, Max pulled Sandy free and hauled him up onto the sled. At once, James and Mandy gently started to pull the sled back until it rested at the edge of the pond. Max clambered off with Sandy in his arms.

"You did it, Max," James said.

But Max's expression was worried. "He's so

cold. We'll have to get him back as quickly as we can."

Mandy unzipped her jacket. "Yours is wet, Max," she explained. "But mine is dry. Sandy will be warmer tucked up in here."

Max put Sandy gently into Mandy's arms, and she zipped her fleecy jacket up around him. "There," she said to the shivering little dog. "Now we have to get you back to Animal Ark as quickly as possible."

Dr. Adam was in the clinic when they arrived. Jean Knox called him at once, then she bundled the children and dogs into the warmth of the living room. A fire blazed cheerfully in the fireplace and the Christmas tree lights were on, but Mandy was too worried to admire them.

They laid Sandy down in front of the fire. The little animal was still shaking with cold, but not quite as much as he had been. Jean brought two big fluffy towels — one for Sandy and one for Max.

"Get that wet jacket off," she said to Max. "You're shivering. Mandy can rub Sandy down while I get her a dry sweater."

Mandy wrapped one of the towels around the little dog, rubbing the warmth back into him, while Max took off his jacket. Underneath, his sweater was also wet.

"I'll get you one of Mandy's," Jean said briskly, going out of the door. "And I've phoned your grandma. She's coming right over."

Mandy finished rubbing Sandy down and changed into a dry sweater. The one she had been wearing was wet all down the front where Sandy had snuggled close to her. Blackie curled up beside Sandy.

"Good boy, Blackie," she murmured to the Labrador. "You're helping to keep him warm, too."

Max dried himself off and slipped on the sweater that Jean brought for him.

"Your dad is coming," Jean said to Mandy. "What on earth happened?"

At that moment Dr. Adam came in, and Mandy explained while her father examined the puppy.

"Well," he said, standing up. "The little fellow seems none the worse for his adventure. You three seem to be turning into a Welford Dog Rescue Team. That's the second pup you've rescued in the last few days!" He looked serious suddenly. "But, you know, that was a very dangerous thing to do, Max."

"It certainly was," added a voice from the door.

Mandy looked around. Mrs. Trigg was standing there in her black coat and hat. Her face was white with worry and she looked angry. "What on earth were you thinking of, Max? You might have been drowned — and all for the sake of that dog. I might have known — animals are nothing but trouble! He'll have to go!" she declared.

Mandy's heart sank. Mrs. Trigg had been growing fond of Sandy, she was sure of it. Now she seemed to hate him more than ever.

Max looked dumbly at his grandmother, with tears in his eyes. Mandy felt suddenly angry. It was so unfair! She could understand how worried and upset Mrs. Trigg was, but she had it all wrong.

"That isn't true, Mrs. Trigg," she burst out. "Sandy was trying to *help* Max."

Mrs. Trigg looked down her nose at Mandy. "Help?" she said. "You call getting itself half drowned and putting Max in danger *helping*?"

"No," said Mandy. "You don't understand. Sandy knew the ice was thin; James and Max will tell you." She turned to the boys. "Remember how Sandy warned Blackie off the ice? He growled and bared his teeth."

"That's right," agreed James. "He had never behaved like that before. We wondered what was wrong."

"Nonsense," Mrs. Trigg said.

"Maybe not, Mrs. Trigg," Dr. Adam cut in. "Dogs have a very keen sense of hearing. If Sandy had heard the ice creaking and beginning to break up, he might have known instinctively that there was danger out there. Go on, Mandy; tell us exactly what Sandy did."

Mandy took a deep breath. "When Max came downhill on his sled, he was heading toward the pool," she explained. "Sandy kept running in front of him, trying to make him change course. Max lost control of his sled and it tipped over and he fell out, but Sandy couldn't stop so he ended up out on the ice. If it hadn't been for Sandy, *Max* would have slid right out onto the ice."

She turned to Mrs. Trigg, looking pleadingly up at her. "So you see, Mrs. Trigg, Sandy saved Max's life. You can't send him away. Anybody can see how much Sandy loves Max, and Max loves Sandy just as much! Max is missing his mom and dad so much, and Sandy is his friend. You *can't* take him away from Max — especially not at Christmastime!"

Mandy stopped, afraid she had gone too far. Mrs. Trigg looked at her for a long moment. Then the old lady looked away, her eyes going around the room. She gazed at the shining

Christmas tree in the window, then her eyes rested on Max and Sandy. Max was sitting in front of the fire with Sandy in his arms. The firelight cast a rosy glow over both of them.

"They certainly seem to love each other," Mrs. Trigg said softly to Mandy. She smiled and went on in a low voice, "It's so Christmassy in here. I remember when my husband was alive we used to have such good Christmases. Oh, how he loved it. He would decorate the cottage from top to bottom, and I would bake a fruit cake — and apple pies, and ginger snaps,

and Christmas cookies. Oh, everything! I haven't bothered about Christmas much since Bill died. Max's mom and dad haven't been able to come for Christmas in recent years, so it hasn't seemed worth it just for myself."

"But it *isn't* just yourself this year, Mrs. Trigg," Mandy said gently.

Mrs. Trigg looked at her in surprise. "You know, you're right, Mandy," she said. "My cottage isn't very Christmassy. Maybe I should do something about that, my dear."

Mandy smiled at the old lady. She wasn't angry after all.

Then Mrs. Trigg spoke briskly. "Let's get you home, Max," she said. "Sandy, too. It seems that I owe him an apology. Perhaps he could sit with us in the living room from now on — but not on the furniture."

Max's face lit up. "Can he lie on the rug in front of the fire? He's had such a shock today. He nearly drowned."

"I think that would be all right," said his grandmother. "Come along now."

"Can I go and see Holly first?" Max asked.

"Holly?" said Mrs. Trigg.

Max nodded. "It's a puppy that Sandy found," he explained. "The poor little thing was abandoned. She would have frozen to death if it hadn't been for Sandy."

Mrs. Trigg smiled. "It seems I've got a lot to learn about Sandy," she said.

"Would *you* like to see Holly, Mrs. Trigg?" Mandy asked.

Mrs. Trigg looked surprised. "Me?" she said. "Why would I want to see a puppy?"

Mandy smiled. "Oh, you might like her," she suggested with a grin.

Mrs. Trigg looked around at the eager faces of the children. "I suppose I might as well have a look," she said after a moment. "After all, what harm can it do?"

Mandy's smile got even wider. "None at all, Mrs. Trigg," she said. "None at all."

8

Mrs. Trigg's Surprise

Mrs. Trigg followed the others into the residential unit. Mandy unlatched Holly's cage and lifted her out. "How are you?" she whispered, cuddling the little puppy.

Holly looked up at her and licked her nose. Mandy giggled.

"We've brought somebody new to see you," James said. "Say hello to Mrs. Trigg, Holly."

Mandy held the puppy out to the old woman. Mrs. Trigg took a step back. "Oh, I don't think I could," she said.

"She's very gentle, Grandma," Max assured his grandmother.

Mrs. Trigg held out her arms slowly and Mandy put the puppy into them. Holly snuggled down and closed her eyes.

"She'll soon be as good as new," Mandy said.

Mrs. Trigg stood quite still, looking at Holly. She was holding the puppy a little awkwardly, but Holly didn't seem to mind. Holly opened her eyes for a moment and nibbled at the old lady's fingers. Mandy tickled the puppy under the chin. "She likes when you do that," she said to Mrs. Trigg.

Mrs. Trigg put a finger under Holly's chin. The puppy looked up at her with big melting eyes and yawned.

"Isn't she adorable?" Max said.

"What exactly happened to her?" Mrs. Trigg asked, looking at Holly's bandage.

Mandy laid her hand lightly on Holly's leg. "Holly was abandoned," she explained. "Mom thinks she was thrown out of a moving car."

Mrs. Trigg looked up, her face shocked. "How dreadful," she said. "How could anyone be so cruel?"

"People do that kind of thing all the time," James said sadly. "But at least Holly was saved."

"Holly . . ." Mrs. Trigg repeated the name. "That's the name of my cottage."

Mandy nodded. "It was Sandy who found her. She had just been left to die in the snow. She was hurt and really cold when we brought her in. If it hadn't been for Sandy, Holly wouldn't be alive now."

Mrs. Trigg looked thoughtful. "It seems that Sandy is quite a clever dog," she remarked.

Mandy nodded. "Oh, he is," she agreed. "And Holly is the sweetest little thing. She has a lovely nature. But she'll have to go to the ASPCA soon."

"And what will happen to her then?" asked Mrs. Trigg, rubbing Holly's ears gently with a finger. Holly snuffled and sneezed. Mrs. Trigg laughed.

"They'll try to find a home for her," Mandy explained. "But it's a difficult time of year. Lots of people get puppies at Christmas and then get rid of them when they find out how much work is involved. There are so many abandoned puppies after Christmas that she might not find a home at all."

"And what would happen then?" asked Mrs. Trigg.

Mandy laid a hand on Holly's furry head and stroked the puppy's nose. "She would have to be put to sleep," she explained.

Mrs. Trigg frowned. "That would be a pity," she said. "Especially after you saved her. She isn't a very young puppy, is she?"

Mandy shook her head. "Holly is about five

months old. She's had all her vaccinations and everything — and she's toilet-trained."

Holly nibbled at Mrs. Trigg's gloved fingers. "I've never thought pets were very useful," she said thoughtfully.

Mandy rubbed Holly's ears. "They *can* be," she said. "Just think about all the guide dogs there are. But the great thing about pets is that they love you and they're good company."

Mrs. Trigg looked even more thoughtful. "That's what Amelia Ponsonby said. Holly seems well enough behaved."

"Holly is *gorgeous*," Mandy declared, burying her face in the puppy's soft coat.

"Hmmph!" said Mrs. Trigg, suddenly brisk. "Well, I can't stand here all day holding a puppy. It's time Max and I went home."

"And Sandy," added Max.

Mrs. Trigg smiled and handed Holly back to Mandy. "And Sandy," she agreed. Mandy and James watched as Mrs. Trigg bundled Max out of the unit.

"Do you think there's any chance of us finding a home for Holly before she has to go to the ASPCA?" James asked.

Mandy looked thoughtful. She was still thinking of the way Mrs. Trigg had held Holly — and she hadn't even bothered to brush off her coat before she left. "You know, James," she said, "I think we might."

On the day before Christmas Eve, Mandy got a surprise telephone call from Mrs. Trigg. "Can you and James come around to see me?" the old lady asked.

"But Max is here at Animal Ark," Mandy said. "He and Sandy are saying good-bye to Holly. She has to go to the ASPCA today," she said sadly.

"I know Max is there," Mrs. Trigg replied. "And I don't want you to tell him you're coming to see me."

"Okay," said Mandy, puzzled. "I'll try to get James alone. He's here, too. We'll both come."

"Make it soon," said Mrs. Trigg mysteriously. "I've got a surprise for Max."

Mandy managed to get James alone and told him about the phone call. "But what are we going to say to Max?" James asked.

Mandy thought for a moment. "What if I ask him to do me a special favor and groom Holly before she goes away?"

"That would work," said James. "Holly certainly loves being groomed. She won't let you stop once you've started."

Mandy grinned and went to find Max. As expected, he was more than willing. He didn't even ask her where she was going.

Mandy and James rushed around to Holly Cottage. Mrs. Trigg was waiting for them and she opened the door at once. James looked at Blackie.

"Should I tie him up outside?" he asked.

Mrs. Trigg shook her head. "Bring him in. Just don't let him jump on the furniture."

James looked at Mandy as they followed Mrs. Trigg into the cottage. Mandy shrugged, then she sniffed. She could smell apple pies baking — and the scent of pine needles. There was something very odd going on at Holly Cottage.

Mrs. Trigg ushered them into the living room and Mandy gasped. There, in the corner of the room, was the prettiest little Christmas tree Mandy had ever seen. It sat in its own pot and its needles were glossy and green. Beside it was a box of lights and tree decorations.

"A Christmas tree!" James exclaimed.

"Do you think Max will like it?" Mrs. Trigg asked anxiously. "It isn't very big."

"It's perfect," James assured her.

"Is that the surprise?" Mandy asked. "Max will love it."

"There's another surprise," Mrs. Trigg said, her eyes shining. "It's wonderful news. I got a call from Max's dad this morning. He and Max's mom *are* going to be here for Christmas after all! Max's mom is coming out of the hospital and his dad has unexpectedly been given a vacation from work. They're arriving later today."

"Oh, that's wonderful," James exclaimed. "Max will be so happy."

"But, don't tell him," Mrs. Trigg warned. "I thought I would have a little surprise party this afternoon to celebrate. It's a long time since I had a Christmas party and *years* since I had a tree. I had forgotten how wonderful a real tree smells."

Mandy smiled with delight, then her face fell.

"What is it, Mandy?" Mrs. Trigg asked.

"Well," Mandy explained, "it's just that we're all going carol singing this afternoon. Max was going to come, too."

Mrs. Trigg pursed her lips. "Well, that's fine," she said at last. "Why don't you all go carol singing and finish up here? Then we can have a party for all the carol singers — and for Max's mom and dad."

"And keep it as a surprise?" asked James.

Mrs. Trigg nodded. "When I saw Animal Ark, I realized how much I'd been missing over these last few years in not making much effort over Christmas. Poor Max; my cottage wasn't very Christmassy for him. I want to make up for that, and a party would make it even more like Christmas."

"But Mrs. Trigg," Mandy said slowly, "you don't understand. The carol singers are all bringing their pets."

"Pets?" repeated Mrs. Trigg.

Mandy nodded. "You know, their dogs and

cats — and Amy Fenton's mouse and Jack Gardiner's rabbit."

"There's even a pony," James put in.

Mrs. Trigg frowned and Mandy's heart sank. There was no way she would want all those animals in her cottage.

"Well," said Mrs. Trigg at last, "I suppose the pony would have to stay outside."

"You mean you would let all the other animals into your cottage?" Mandy squeaked.

Mrs. Trigg looked around her living room. It was bright and cheerful, and not quite as tidy as usual. There were more Christmas decorations spilling out of a box, which was sitting on a chair, and a pile of presents waiting to be wrapped. "I can always clean it up afterward," she said. "After all, I like a chance to give the cottage a good cleaning."

Mandy and James looked at each other and laughed.

"Mrs. Trigg," said James pointing to the box on the chair, "would you like us to help you put those decorations up?"

"That would be wonderful, James," Mrs. Trigg replied.

Mandy rolled up her sleeves. "Okay, where do you want them?" she asked.

Mrs. Trigg spread her arms wide. "*Everywhere*, Mandy!"

9

A Home for Holly

Mandy had a lot to think about while she and James helped Mrs. Trigg with her decorations. As they left Holly Cottage, she grabbed James's arm. "James," she said, "do you think *Mrs. Trigg* would take Holly?"

James looked at Mandy in surprise. "Mrs. Trigg?" he exclaimed. "I know she really likes

Sandy — deep down. But would she really want a puppy of her own?"

"She's changed such a lot," Mandy said thoughtfully. "I can't help thinking of the way she looked at Holly. I'm sure she liked her."

James shoved his glasses up on his nose.

"Well, we haven't got much time if we're going to try," he said. "Holly will be leaving Animal Ark pretty soon."

"So, let's go," Mandy said. "We've got to ask Mom and Dad."

"I hope we'll get there in time," Mandy gasped as they rushed up the path and into the clinic. They almost collided with Mandy's grandma, who was just coming out of the door.

"What's all the hurry?" Grandma asked.

"Grandma, has Dad left with Holly yet?" Mandy gasped.

"He's just fetching her now. You'll be in time to say a last good-bye."

"Maybe we won't have to," Mandy said hurriedly. "Oh, Grandma, Mrs. Trigg is going to have a surprise party for Max. His mom and dad are coming home today and she wants the carol singers to go to Holly Cottage after we finish. She's decorating the cottage and baking and — everything."

"Well, well," said Grandma. "I'm glad to hear that. I met her yesterday and she was looking a lot more like her old self." Then Grandma paused. "Do you think she could use a bit of help to get ready for the party?"

"I'm sure she could," Mandy said, smiling. "Grandma, you're great!"

"You're not so bad yourself," Grandma said to Mandy as she rushed into Animal Ark. "I'll go there right away."

Dr. Adam was lifting Holly out of her cage. Dr. Emily was with him and so was Max.

"Dad," Mandy gasped, "can we keep Holly just a little while longer?"

Dr. Adam frowned. "But we agreed that she should go to the ASPCA today."

"Maybe we won't have to send her at all," James burst out.

Dr. Emily smiled. "Now, slow down," she said. "What's all this about?"

"I think I've found a home for Holly," Mandy explained. "I'm almost sure that Mrs. Trigg would take her."

"Grandma?" Max cried.

Mandy nodded. "She's so much nicer to Sandy now, Max. You know that. And she really liked Holly when she met her — I know she did."

Dr. Emily looked thoughtful. "You said *almost* sure, Mandy," she said. "Haven't you asked her? It's a big risk to take. You know that after Christmas there will be lots more puppies for the ASPCA to find homes for. At least if she goes today, there'll be a slight chance that somebody might choose her as a pet before Christmas."

Mandy nodded. "I know that, Mom," she said. "But it isn't a very big chance, and I just know that if Mrs. Trigg sees Holly again she'll change her mind about having a pet. And it would mean that Holly could stay in Welford. Please — can I try? Please?"

Dr. Adam and Dr. Emily looked at each other. Mandy gazed at the little puppy in her father's arms. She couldn't bear to lose Holly, entirely.

"I suppose it's worth a try," Dr. Adam said at last. "But you mustn't force Mrs. Trigg to take her, Mandy."

"Oh, we wouldn't do that," said James.

Max grinned. "They *couldn't* force Grandma," he said. "If she says yes, it's because she really wants Holly."

Mandy laid a hand on Holly's silky coat. Max had groomed the little terrier-cross until she gleamed. "Of course she wants Holly," she declared. "She just doesn't *know* it yet!"

Dr. Emily smiled. "All right then, Mandy," she said. "But if Mrs. Trigg *doesn't* want Holly, then she'll have to go tomorrow morning. We can't keep her."

Mandy nodded, her face serious again. "I know that, Mom," she said. "But I'm sure I'm right. I'm just sure of it."

Mandy looked at Max. Now all she had to do was keep him at Animal Ark for the afternoon, so that the party would be a surprise. "Let's practice some carols," she suggested, nudging James. "Then we can all go out singing from here."

"Good idea," said James, taking the hint. "Come on, Max. Let's get the carol sheets."

Mandy looked at James gratefully as he

dragged Max out of the door. "I've got another surprise," she announced to her mom and dad, and launched into explanations about the party.

"*Good King Wenceslas looked out
On the feast of Stephen . . .*"

The carol rang around the village as Mandy and her friends sang, walking up the snowy main street. Even the animals were joining in. Duchess meowed along with the music and Blackie gave a bark. Paddy had tinsel threaded through his bridle and a warm red blanket on his back. He whinnied softly. All over the village, people came to their doors to hear the carols.

Mandy was carrying Holly in her arms. Her leg was no longer bandaged, but Mandy wanted to be quite sure the little animal came to no harm. The puppy looked up as a flake of snow settled on her nose. More flakes fell, shining in the light of the lamps the children carried. They only had one more house to go now and, as they approached Holly Cottage, Mandy cuddled Holly closer to her. "Not long now, Holly. You'll soon have a new home, I promise you," she whispered to the puppy.

James opened the gate of Holly Cottage and Jill Redfern started a new carol: "*Ding dong merrily on high . . .*"

They all joined in, the sound floating through the frosty air toward the front door. It opened, flooding the path with light. Mrs. Trigg stood there waiting for them.

The children grouped themselves around the door and finished the carol. Max was flushed with pleasure.

Mrs. Trigg beamed at them. "That was lovely," she said. "Thank you! Now, come in out of the cold. I've got a surprise for you all."

The children trooped into the house. "Take your shoes off," Mrs. Trigg ordered, but she said it with a smile.

Paul tied Paddy to the front porch, making sure the pony was protected from the snow.

Leaving their boots and coats in the hall, the

carol singers followed Mrs. Trigg to the living room. Mandy gasped. The tree twinkled in the corner, the room was festooned with decorations, and a fire burned brightly in the hearth. But it wasn't the decorations that made her gasp — it was the table, laden with goodies. Along with plates full of delicious-looking tiny sandwiches and rolls, there were others heaped with pies, gingerbread, and little iced cupcakes. A beautifully decorated fruit cake sat in the middle.

"Grandma!" breathed Max.

I thought you would like a party for your friends," Mrs. Trigg told him. "Mandy and James helped me keep it a surprise for you. And Mandy's grandma helped with the baking. She even brought around a spare fruit cake she'd baked, as I didn't have time to bake one. We had great fun decorating it this afternoon!"

"But what about all the *animals*?" Max asked.

Mrs. Trigg looked around the little choir. Timmy, Peter Foster's cairn terrier, bounded up to the table and looked longingly at the goodies. Jack Gardiner's rabbit, Hoppy, poked his head around Jack's arm and waggled his ears, and Amy Fenton's mouse, Minnie, twitched her whiskers.

"Don't worry," said Amy. "I won't let her go. She doesn't like Duchess much." The furry Persian cat stalked over to the table and meowed.

Mrs. Trigg laughed. "Just keep them off the furniture," she said. "There are lots of nice things for the pets, too — in the kitchen."

"What about Paddy?" asked Paul.

"There are carrots and apples," Mrs. Trigg told him. "Paddy can share them with Jack's rabbit."

Max was looking as if he couldn't believe his ears. Just then the doorbell rang. Mandy's mom and dad trooped in with Grandma and Grandpa.

"Now the party can really start," said Mrs. Trigg happily. "Come on then — dig in!"

They didn't need to be told twice. Grandma beamed at Mrs. Trigg. "I was just saying to

Tom that we'll have to get you back on the committee of the Women's Club, Maggie," she said. "We could do with a good cook like you to help with all our functions."

Mrs. Trigg flushed. "Oh, Dorothy, I would really like that," she said, her face lighting up.

Mandy was halfway through a plate of egg sandwiches and apple pie when Mrs. Trigg came over to her. Holly was sitting quietly at Mandy's feet. Mandy bent and fed her a bit of sandwich, then picked the little dog up with one hand, balancing her plate in the other.

"This is the puppy that was abandoned, isn't it?" Mrs. Trigg asked.

Mandy nodded innocently. "You'd better say good-bye to her, Mrs. Trigg," she said. "I was hoping somebody in Welford would adopt her. She's so sweet. I'll really miss her when she goes. It's such a pity she can't stay here among her friends."

"You'd think *somebody* would want her," Mrs. Trigg said. "Just look at her beautiful coat."

"She loves being groomed," Mandy continued, watching Mrs. Trigg run her hand
through Holly's silky hair.

"She's a lovely little thing," Mrs. Trigg said.

"I hope she finds a good home." Mandy sighed
and deliberately tipped her plate just a little.
"Can you take her for a moment, Mrs. Trigg?"
she asked. "I don't want to spill anything."

Mrs. Trigg put out her arms and gathered the
little puppy into them. "I'm not very good
with animals," she said.

Mandy looked at the old lady cradling the
puppy. Holly put her head in the crook of Mrs.
Trigg's arm and yawned. "Oh, I think you are,"
Mandy said softly. "Holly likes you."

Mrs. Trigg looked down at the puppy won-
deringly. "Do you really think so?" she asked.

The doorbell rang again. Mrs. Trigg went to
answer it. A man and woman came into the
room, shaking the snow from their coats.

"Oops, sorry about the mess, Mom," the
man said, hugging Mrs. Trigg. "We were in a
rush to see Max."

"Come in! Come in!" Mrs. Trigg welcomed them, her eyes sparkling with happiness. "Max, here's another surprise for you."

"Dad! *Mom!*" Max yelled, flying across the room. "How did you get here, Dad? Are you better now, Mom?"

Max's mom held out her arms and Max hugged her while she explained how she got out of the hospital early.

"And I got all my work finished early, too, Max," his father explained, ruffling his son's hair. "Mom and I wanted so much to be with you for Christmas."

Max turned, his arms around both his parents. "What a Christmas present!" he said.

His mom looked around. "Oh, you're having a party," she said, looking surprised.

Max's dad grinned. "Look at all these animals, Mom," he said. "This is great. Max won't want to come home with us after Christmas if he's been having such a good time here!"

Max looked at his grandma. "Grandma has

been great," he said. "She's been really kind to Sandy."

Mrs. Trigg blushed. "Oh, I don't know about that, Max," she said. "I wasn't very good with him at first."

"That doesn't matter now," Max said. "Sandy thinks you're great."

Sandy scampered across the room and tried to untie Mrs. Trigg's shoelaces. "Down, Sandy," Mrs. Trigg said, but she was smiling. "That's his favorite game!" she said.

Sandy sat down and looked up at her, wagging his tail.

"And you've got a dog of your own," Max's mom said, coming over to stand beside her mother-in-law and stroking the puppy in her arms.

"Oh, no . . ." Mrs. Trigg began.

"Good for you, Mom," her son said. "I've thought for a long while that you should get a pet to keep you company, and a dog is perfect. What's its name?"

"Holly," said Mrs. Trigg, looking confused.

"Just like the cottage," Max's mom said, smiling. She had soft brown hair and blue eyes — like Max.

"But she isn't mine," said Mrs. Trigg.

Mandy looked up at her. "She *could* be, though," she said gently.

Mrs. Trigg looked down at the puppy in her arms. Holly opened her eyes and gazed adoringly back, then she licked Mrs. Trigg's hand.

Mandy waited, holding her breath.

"Do you think she would *like* to stay at Holly Cottage with me?" Mrs. Trigg asked.

"I'm sure she would," Mandy replied. "You'd be rescuing her, Mrs. Trigg."

"And she would be such good company," Mrs. Trigg answered. "I think I'm going to miss Sandy when he goes."

"I'll bring Sandy to see Holly lots of times," Max promised. "They're good friends."

Mrs. Trigg looked around at all the eager faces. "I'd love to have her! What an unexpected Christmas gift!" she said.

"And you've given Holly the best Christmas

present as well," Mandy assured her. "A home!" She looked across at her mom and dad; they were both smiling. Dr. Adam gave her the thumbs-up sign.

"You've given *me* the best Christmas ever, Grandma," said Max. "I've never had such a good party."

Mandy and James looked at each other. "A pets' party," Mandy declared. "The best party possible!"

Make a New Friend!

Whenever a pet is in trouble, Mandy Hope and her friend James are ready to help.

Read about their adventures in a very special series.

ANIMAL ARK PETS™

by Ben M. Baglio

☐ BDD 0-439-05158-4   #1: Puppy Puzzle
☐ BDD 0-439-05159-2   #2: Kitten Crowd
☐ BDD 0-439-05160-6   #3: Rabbit Race
☐ BDD 0-439-05161-4   #4: Hamster Hotel
☐ BDD 0-439-05162-2   #5: Mouse Magic
☐ BDD 0-439-05163-0   #6: Chick Challenge
☐ BDD 0-439-05164-9   #7: Pony Parade
☐ BDD 0-439-05165-7   #8: Guinea Pig Gang
☐ BDD 0-439-05166-5   #9: Gerbil Genius
☐ BDD 0-439-05167-3   #10: Duckling Diary
☐ BDD 0-439-05168-1   #11: Lamb Lesson
☐ BDD 0-439-05169-X   #12: Doggy Dare
☐ BDD 0-439-05170-3   #13: Cat Crazy
☐ BDD 0-439-23023-3   #14: Ferret Fun
☐ BDD 0-439-23024-1   #15: Bunny Bonanza
☐ BDD 0-439-23025-X   #16: Frog Friends

$3.99 US EACH

Available wherever you buy books, or use this order form.

Scholastic Inc., P.O. Box 7502, Jefferson City, MO 65102

Please send me the books I have checked above. I am enclosing $_____ (please add $2.00 to cover shipping and handling). Send check or money order—no cash or C.O.D.s please.

Name _____ Age _____

Address _____

City _____ State/Zip _____

Please allow four to six weeks for delivery. Offer good in the U.S. only. Sorry, mail orders are not available to residents of Canada. Prices subject to change.

AAP